This edition specially produced for Heritage Books
by HarperCollins Publishers Ltd in 2002
ISBN 0-00-761345-8
Reprinted in 2004

6 8 10 9 7 5

First published in hardback in Great Britain in 1992
First published in Picture Lions in 1994
Picture Lions is an imprint of the Children's Division, part of HarperCollins
Publishers Ltd, 77-85 Fulham Palace Road, Hammersmith, London W6 8JB.

A CIP catalogue for this title is available from the British Library.

Printed and bound in Hong Kong.

Paddington at the Tower

Michael Bond

Illustrated by John Lobban

THE TOWER OF LONDON

Soon after Paddington went to live at number thirty-two Windsor Gardens Mr and Mrs Brown gave him a basket on wheels.

The Browns' house was near the Portobello Road, where there was a large market, and every morning Paddington went there to do his shopping.

After calling at the baker's, where he had a standing order for buns, he then went on to see his friend Mr Gruber, who kept an antique shop.

Paddington liked Mr Gruber's shop. It was so full of things it was like Aladdin's cave.

Every day Mr Gruber made some cocoa and they had their "elevenses" together.

One morning, however, Paddington had a surprise.
When he reached the shop he found Mr Gruber busy
putting up his shutters.

"It's Easter Monday, Mr Brown," he said. "And
as it's such a nice day I thought I would take you
and Jonathan and Judy on a mystery outing."

Paddington was very excited. He hurried back home to tell the others and then he began making some marmalade sandwiches. He soon had so many he could hardly close the lid of his suitcase.

Later that morning they set off, and Mr Gruber found them a seat right at the front of the bus so that he could point out the interesting sights on the way.

They had been travelling for quite a while when Jonathan and Judy suddenly let out a cry.

"I know where we're going," said Judy, as they turned a corner.

"It's the Tower of London!" exclaimed Jonathan.

Paddington had never been to the Tower of London before and he was most impressed. It was much, much bigger than he had pictured.

As they reached the entrance a man in a strange uniform stepped forward to take their tickets.

"That's one of the Beefeaters," whispered Jonathan. "They look after the Tower."

"They're really Yeoman Warders," explained Judy. "But they get called Beefeaters because in the old days they used to taste all the royal food to make sure it was safe to eat."

Paddington raised his hat politely and then opened his suitcase.

"Would you like one of my marmalade sandwiches?" he asked. "I expect it will make a nice change from beef."

"A marmalade sandwich!" spluttered the Beefeater. He held the object up between his thumb and forefinger and stared at it as if he could hardly believe his eyes.

But when he looked down again Paddington had gone.

Taking one look at the expression on the man's face, he picked up his suitcase and hurried after the others. Several more sandwiches dropped out on the way, but by then he was much too upset to notice.

Mr Gruber hastily led them through an arch. When they were safely round the corner he stopped beside a large cage.

"This is where they keep the ravens, Mr Brown," he said.

"They've always had ravens here and it's said that if they ever fly away, then the Tower will fall down."

Paddington peered at the empty cage. "Perhaps we'd better go soon, Mr Gruber," he said anxiously.

Mr Gruber laughed. "I don't think there's any fear of it happening just yet, Mr Brown," he said. "That Tower looks very solid to me."

He pointed towards a large black bird standing watching them. "Besides, there's at least one raven keeping an eye on things."

"He looks as if he's got his eye on Paddington," said Judy.

Next, Mr Gruber took them to a room deep under the ground.

"This is where the Crown Jewels are kept," whispered Judy. "They are made of gold and they are very valuable. That's why they are kept behind glass."

Mr Gruber showed them the St Edward's Crown...

...the Orb and Sceptre

...and an Ampula and Spoon for holy oil.

"They were all used by the Queen at her Coronation," he explained. "The crown has over four hundred precious stones and it weighs nearly five pounds!"

Paddington's eyes grew larger and larger. He could quite see why no-one wanted the Tower to fall down.

When they came out of the Jewel House Paddington noticed a strange thing. There were now two ravens watching him.

A moment later two more arrived, and all four stared at him as he went past.

Paddington gave them a hard stare back, but
for once it didn't seem to have any effect.

"Perhaps we'd better have our picnic outside by the
river," said Judy, when she saw the worried look on
Paddington's face. "They won't follow you out there."

But the ravens did follow Paddington, and by the time they reached the gate there were so many he'd nearly lost count.

"And where do you think you are going with our ravens, young fellow-me-bear?" asked the Beefeater in charge.

"*He's* not going anywhere with them," said Jonathan and Judy. "*They're* going with him."

"It makes no difference," said the man sternly. "I'm not letting them leave here and risk having the place fall down. That bear will have to stay in the Tower until we've decided what's best."

"Oh, crikey!" groaned Jonathan. "Fancy Paddington being sent to the Tower."

Suddenly Mr Gruber had an idea. "You know what?" he said excitedly. "I don't think it's Mr Brown they're after at all. I think it's his sandwiches!"

Paddington gazed at Mr Gruber in astonishment. "My sandwiches!" he exclaimed hotly.

But Mr Gruber was right. Sure enough, as soon as Paddington opened his suitcase all the ravens gathered round and began pecking at the contents.

"All the years I've been here," said the Beefeater, "and I never knew ravens liked marmalade."

He looked at Paddington with new respect. "Perhaps you could give me your address, sir. Then if any of our birds ever get lost we can send for you.

"We may even be able to find you a special jar of marmalade to keep by you in case it's needed in a hurry."

"Trust Paddington to get sent to the Tower and then end up with a jar of marmalade!" exclaimed Judy.

Paddington looked at it happily. "If I'm to be a Marmalade-eater," he announced, "perhaps I'd better test it now – just to make sure!"